AESOP'S FABLES

The Wolf in Sheep's Clothing

RETOLD BY MARY BERENDES • ILLUSTRATED BY NANCY HARRISON

Distributed by The Child's World®
1980 Lookout Drive • Mankato, MN 56003-1705
800-599-READ • www.childsworld.com

ACKNOWLEDGMENTS
The Child's World®: Mary Berendes, Publishing Director
The Design Lab: Art Direction and Design
Red Line Editorial: Editing

LIBRARY OF CONGRESS CATALOGING-IN-PUBLICATION DATA
Berendes, Mary.
 The wolf in sheep's clothing / by Mary Berendes ; illustrated by Nancy
Harrison.
    p. cm. — (Aesop's fables)
 Summary: A retelling of Aesop's fable about a hungry, but unlucky, wolf who
tries to capture a tasty lamb for dinner by disguising himself in sheep's wool.
 ISBN 978-1-60253-527-5 (library bound : alk. paper)
 [1. Fables. 2. Folklore.] I. Harrison, Nancy, 1963– ill. II. Aesop. III. Title.
IV. Series.
 PZ8.2.B46925Wol 2010
 398.2—dc22
 [E]   2010009975

Printed in the United States of America in Mankato, Minnesota.
July 2010
F11538

Beware of a wolf in sheep's clothing: things are not always what they appear to be.

Every night, a hungry wolf would prowl around a flock of sheep. But every night, the shepherd and his dogs would find the wolf and chase him away.

One day, the wolf found a
sheep's fleece that had fallen
off a wagon going to market.
The wolf pulled the fleece over
his head.

He tucked his fur in so that none of it showed under the fleece. Now the wolf looked just like a sheep!

The wolf strolled among the flock. The shepherd never noticed him. The dogs never barked. The wolf now looked just like all the other sheep.

Now that he was among the flock, the wolf could catch his meal! Now each night the wolf would sneak off into the forest with a tasty sheep.

The wolf grew quite fat on his many meals. He became the fattest sheep in the flock!

One day, the shepherd decided to cook a sheep for his dinner.

He chose the biggest, fattest sheep he could find. Can you guess which sheep he chose?

AESOP

Aesop was a storyteller who lived more than 2,500 years ago. He lived so long ago, there isn't much information about him. Most people believe Aesop was a slave who lived in the area around the Mediterranean Sea—probably in or near the country of Greece.

Aesop's fables are known in almost every culture in the world, in almost every language. His fables are even *part* of some languages! Some common phrases come from Aesop's fables, such as "sour grapes" and "Never count your chickens before they've hatched."

ABOUT FABLES

Fables are one of the oldest forms of stories. They are often short and funny, and have animals as the main characters. These animals act like people. Often, fables teach the reader a lesson. This is called a *moral*. A moral might teach right from wrong, or show how to act in good, kind ways. A moral might show what happens when someone makes a poor decision. Fables teach us how to live wisely.

Mary Berendes has authored dozens of books for children, including nature titles as well as books about countries and holidays. She loves to collect antique books and has some that are almost 200 years old. Mary lives in Minnesota.

Nancy Harrison was born and raised in Montreal. She has worked as an art director, creative director, and advertising executive with clients all over the world. After relocating to Philadelphia, she began working as a freelance illustrator. Nancy's work has been published in dozens of magazines and over 30 children's books. Nancy currently lives in Vermont.